D0116959

I just jump in the lake.

I just jump with my brother Jake.

Jump!

The Sound of J

by Cynthia Klingel and Robert B. Noyed

The Child's World®, Inc.

I just jump down the street.

I just jump on my feet.

I just jump up so high.

I just jump to reach
the sky.

I just jump in the sand.

I just jump on the land.

I just jump and sing
a song.

I just jump all day long.

Word List

Jake

jump

just

Note to Parents and Educators

The books in the Phonics series of the Wonder Books are based on current research which supports the idea that our brains are pattern detectors rather than rules appliers. This means children learn to read easier when they are taught the familiar spelling patterns found in English. As children encounter more complex words, they have greater success in figuring out these words by using the spelling patterns.

Throughout the 35 books, the texts provide the reader with the opportunity to practice and apply knowledge of the sounds in natural language. The 10 books on the long and short vowels introduce the sounds using familiar onsets and rimes, or spelling patterns, for reinforcement. For example, the word "cat" might be used to present the short "a" sound, with the letter "c" being the onset and "-at" being the rime. This approach provides practice and reinforcement of the short "a" sound, as there are many familiar words made with the "-at" rime.

The 21 consonants and the 4 blends ("ch," "sh," "th," and "wh") use many of these same rimes. The letter(s) before the vowel in a word are considered the onset. Changing the onset allows the consonant books in the series to maintain the practice and reinforcement of the rimes. The repeated use of a word or phrase reinforces the target sound.

The number on the spine of each book facilitates arranging the books in the order that children acquire each sound. The books can also be arranged into groups of long vowels, short vowels, consonants, and blends. All the books in each grouping have their numbers printed in the same color on the spine. The books can be grouped and regrouped easily and quickly, depending on the teacher's needs.

The stories and accompanying photographs in this series are based on time-honored concepts in children's literature: Well-written, engaging texts and colorful, high-quality photographs combine to produce books that children want to read again and again.

Dr. Peg Ballard
Minnesota State University, Mankato

Photo Credits

All photos © copyright: PhotoEdit: 18 (Richard Hutchings); Tony Stone Images: 5 (Jerome Tisne), 6 (Bill Robbins), 10, 13 (Peter Cade), 14 (Donald Nausbaum), 17 (Nicole Katano); Unicorn Stock Photos: 2 (Jeff Greenberg), 9 (Tom McCarthy), 20 (Kimberly Burnham). Cover: Tony Stone Images/Peter Cade.

Photo Research: Alice Flanagan
Design and production: Herman Adler Design Group

Library of Congress Cataloging-in-Publication Data

Klingel, Cynthia Fitterer.
    Jump! : the sound of "j" / by Cynthia Klingel and Robert B. Noyed.
      p. cm. — (Wonder books)
    Summary : Simple text and repetition of the letter "j" help readers learn how to use this sound.
    ISBN 1-56766-696-5 (lib. bdg. : alk. paper)
    [1. Alphabet. 2. Stories in rhyme.] I. Noyed, Robert B. II. Title.
    III. Series: Wonder books (Chanhassen, Minn.)
    PZ8.3.K683Ju   1999
    [E]—dc21
                                         99-20960
                                            CIP